DARK NIGHT STORIES
TO SCARE KIDS

Dark Night Stories to Scare Kids

WARDAN STANLO WISCHOWSKI

WanderingSpiritMWarrior

Preface

These stories are gathered from many places around North America. Whenever possible the stories were investigated to confirm and as much as can be verified, they are true. We have substituted out the real names, but not the real events. The blackness is out there for whomever is willing to see.

Do Not Call
Her Name

Do Not Call Her Name

When Jorge, age 10, moved into his creepy new townhome with his mom, it wasn't brand new. One family had lived there before. But no one died in it. Before it was a townhome, there was a regular house on that land. No one died in that house either. Before that modern house was a very old house. No one ever died in that old house. But before that old house, there was a log cabin, when no other houses and streets were around, just orchards stretching as far as you could see. And that is when someone died in that place, so long ago that it was before hospitals and ambulances. We'll never know how the little girl died because it was before detailed news and record keeping... but we know her name. Jorge's strange experience matches the name in the obituary.

For weeks Jorge was pestered by strange feelings and seeing things... at night... in the home. No dust built up in his room. Something in the night dusted everything. He could see it if he watched. It threw away his new electronic toys and kept pulling his old teddy bears and blocks out of his closet. It sat on his stomach and pulled his toes. And he would wake up in the night and could smell a person's breath, gross breath, like they ate oatmeal and cornbread and forgot to brush. He smelled it when no one was there.

She was never around in the daytime, only at night, only in the dark. He could see her long curly hair disappear around a corner or the ruffles of her dress coming in and out of a moon ray, but never all of her at once. That is until he started to dream about her. In the beginning the dreams were all different and crazy, but the dreams started to all become exactly the same. They would be playing blocks together, but as soon as he took one of her blocks to use, she killed him. He would try not to take her block; he would try to find another block or just not build anything. But every time in the dream it turned out the same; he took one little block and she killed him.

She was always spelling something with her blocks. Normally in a dream you can't read; you can imagine reading, but you can't really see the words. It's a trick of how the brain and dreaming works. But Jorge had the dream so much that he started to remember the letters on the blocks when he was awake. After weeks of torture he could remember all the blocks. They said, "Julia Anne."

Jorge worried all day at school, but thought maybe he had found the answer. Maybe he could free the ghost, like her name was the key to the spell. When it was dark, good and dark, he went to his room. He kept the light off. He pulled all of his blocks out of the closet, but he didn't play with them himself, he played with his old teddy bears and waited. He was going to talk to her and solve his problem.

She didn't play at first. She dusted everything. She had to finish her chores before she could play. He tried to wait, but when she seemed to be finished dusting she didn't come to the blocks yet. So he tried to say her name. He said, "Julia Anne."

Instantly she rushed his face like a monster, making a gruesome hiss scowl. He screamed and tried to run away and that's all he could remember.

He woke up in the hospital. He had a bloody bump on his head. He didn't know if she hit him or he ran into something because he was so scared. But he didn't say her name at night in that home anymore.

Jorge already had no real friends at school. The stress had made him sickly and bony and it was disturbing to the other kids. Now with a big scabby bump, even the teacher couldn't really stand to look at him. She had to think of something else to look at whenever she talked to him. Only one kid still took an interest in Jorge, so that one kid was his only "friend". The truth is, Lincoln was fascinated by Jorge's morphing into a sub-human creature. Lincoln was the only one who would still play with Jorge, and the only one who would listen, so Jorge mistook that for caring. Jorge told Lincoln everything; he told him, the name... "Julia Anne". Lincoln asked to come over and play after school.

Jorge strictly warned Lincoln to not say the name, but the first thing Lincoln did before he even got through the door was to start saying it, all across the front yard. Over and over, every ten minutes he had to say it again. Lincoln thought it was hilarious and fascinating. Jorge was so angry, but she wasn't coming out. Jorge began to believe he was safe, that it had been a mistake. He was more grateful to Lincoln for freeing him. Lincoln was his real friend.

Lincoln stayed too late. He had dinner with Jorge and his mom. After dinner it was dark. Lincoln said her name in the dark.

The mother knows there was some kind of struggle, but both boys gave conflicting and mostly incoherent versions of what happened, statements mentioning ghosts, boogeymen, and apparently vampires. The investigators believe the boys barely survived with the help of friendship, but cannot make out the boys' statements any better than the mother. Whatever really happened, the mother finally moved, new school, new everything, except no more wooden blocks, that's for sure. She burned those nightmare blocks in the driveway and she got a ticket for it, but she didn't care. She just wanted her boy to be free.

But the end of our records show that Jorge died soon in the next home. The mother refused to cooperate with journalists and the results of the police investigation were kept confidential. Police reports are rarely helpful for this kind of thing anyway. There's no way to know, but we're afraid the boy called her name again, and that Julia Anne isn't truly bound to that one home, just the darkness.

You can write her name all you want, and say it in the light, but since there is always darkness somewhere, for the sake that you may be too near to some darkness, for the sake of keeping safety first, do not call her name.

Georgian
Lantern

Georgian Lantern

This story is not true, but I just can't resist including it. We tried tracking down the original author of the story, but it's impossible. Nearly every small midwestern town we contacted claimed the origin of the story. But none of the stories vary on one key point—it's always the Georgian Lantern.

A mysterious package always arrives at town hall. It doesn't have a proper return address, just Georgia. The town clerk always opens it to find an old tin lantern inside. And no one in all the town hall can think of who would send an old lantern or whom they'd send it to. But by and by they remember how the gravedigger seems to dig all alone at night, and in nothing but the moon and starlight. So they leave that bygone lantern hanging in the cemetery's old dead "Widow's Tree" and forget all about it.

***

Back in the olden days it was important for kids to have rights of passage as they grew up. Some of these were invented by parents, but some were invented by kids, usually to prove how brave (maybe crazy) they were. And in really small communities, where all the parents knew one another and grew up in the same place, these strange rituals might become part of the local tradition, unofficially, of course. In this unknown town the right of passage for a boy who didn't want to be treated like a baby was to spend the night in the cemetery. Parents let this happen because it was tradition. The dads had to do it, so why shouldn't their sons do it too? (I don't know what the girls did.) A boy didn't stay by himself. He just had to spend the WHOLE night camping in the cemetery with one older boy as a witness. In this story it was two brothers. The little brother was ready to claim his big boy title, and his big brother was obliged to stay with him whether he felt like it or not.

When the boys got there to stay the night, a little after sunset, they had sleeping bags and snacks, but no lights. It was against the rules to bring your own lights. There was no rule against using a light you found there already. They sure felt lucky. Really no light at all would have been better. Without knowing the origin of the Georgian Lantern, no one can really say-- is it witchcraft or aliens? But whatever made it, it's sure that the Georgian lantern is not natural. The light that it gives off is harmless, kind of, except that the shadows cast by the Georgian lantern grow into evil things, things that come alive.

As the twilight darkened, the shadows darkened, and as the shadows darkened they became stronger. And when they were strong enough, they moved. Now this little brother knew that the first thing "babies" do is to see shadows moving in the night and to start imagining a monster. So he knew that to not be a "baby" he had to ignore that nonsense. *Just forget those things you keep noticing in the corners of your eyes and the back of your mind.* For the big brother it was a little different. He was too old for seeing shadows move. When he started feeling like he saw the shadows move, he reassured himself that the neighborhood boys were just hiding around and pranking them.

The big brother waited. He had to leave his little brother to deal with it. If the big brother chased off the neighborhood bullies, then they would argue that the little brother hadn't braved it on his own and didn't pass. They'd treat him like a baby and he'd be stuck doing the whole thing over again. He saw his little brother staring at a shadow. He egged it on just... just because it's what a big brother is supposed to do.

"Are you afraid of the shadows, little baby? Are you gonna cry?"

The little brother answered calmly and nobly, "Tsk, I know they're not monsters. You aren't scaring me."

So the big brother lost his patience with the neighborhood jerks and went ahead and shouted it out, "He already knows it's you guys, you aren't scaring us!"

There was no response. No one came out from hiding and gave up. No one made one last try of shouting "Boo!" There was just a little bit of laughing, but it didn't sound like his friends' voices. It also sounded like the laughing voices were inside the cemetery fence. They shouldn't be inside. Nobody was allowed inside with them. Besides, the brothers had closed the gate and you could hear when that rusty gate opened from two blocks away. And you wouldn't climb that fence. It was high and topped with decorative spear tips from more older days when grave robbing was a common thing. No, for sure, echoes or something must have made the voices sound close. No one could be inside the gates.

The brothers decided to go to the fence and look around. At the farthest part of the fence all shadows from the Georgian lantern seemed to bend and distort. They both felt just a crazy little thought as if the fence were trying to bend its spear tips at them. Then they started rubbing their eyes hard because the cast shadow of the fence didn't match the fence itself; it was bent all different. And some things started coming out of that cast shadow, like little clawed hands reaching out, and barbed devils' tails waving around.

"Let's go back to the light," said the big brother, thinking the light would keep them safer from evil. The idea of "evil" had gotten into the big brother's head even.

But when they turned around, all over the cemetery shadows were coming alive. It was still in the style of one of those old-fashioned graveyards where most of the tombstones stand up from the ground. All those tall slabs of marble or granite, and crosses too, cast so darned many shadows. And, to make it worse, every single shadow seemed to have eyes peeking out and clawed fingers reaching over.

They ran back to the light and when they did, one small tombstone was scarier than the rest. Some giant yellow eyes appeared peeking over it. Those big, slimy, yellow eyes peeked more and more and seemed to get bigger as they came over the stone. This funny kind of shiny, black creature was staring at them while all the other hidden creatures still hid and laughed. The little black creature peeked around the side and started to emerge. It was mostly head, with a little, runty body and short legs. The arms were somewhat long with long fingers and claws. But those creepy arms were still small compared to that big head with the huge eyes and the broad mouth. It started shuffling up to them with its tiny feet. They backed against the Widow's Tree, hoping the light would protect them, but Georgian Lantern light doesn't protect you from Georgian shadow evil. And what's worse is the lamp was hung in the tree, so while the most light was there, shadows were crisscrossed around all the branches of the tree. The Widow's Tree came to life, started wriggling its branches, and grabbed them up even as they pressed against it for safety.

But the tree didn't pick them right up and lift them up high; it tortured them. It held them just this little bit off the ground so that as they struggled and kicked, they kept feeling their feet touch the ground. It felt like they could only just get traction a little and then run away. Sure, the gate was heavy and always got stuck, but a bad chance at running away was better than no chance. They didn't care if their clothes got torn or their faces got scratched. They just kept kicking and wiggling, crazy to get their feet on the ground, while the little black monster came closer. They started to give up kicking and stared in terror. The little monster started to smile and, as its lips parted, it showed these shining and horribly perfect, white, sharp, sharp teeth.

The really unsettling thing about the creature was the way its teeth filled its mouth. To begin with they all fit together in a perfect zigzag. But by some kind of alien monster magic, as its jaw got farther open, instead of the teeth getting farther apart too, they just kept getting bigger. The mouth was so wide, from one side of the head to the other, and just spreading a grin into more and more teeth. It was like nothing but eyes and teeth coming at them.

When he got close he stopped. He looked from one brother to the other. They knew he was deciding which one to eat first. At first he thought that he would eat the big brother first so that the little brother would feel all the extra terror of knowing his big brother couldn't rescue him. It's as if that terror would make the boy juicier and better tasting for the monster. But then the little monster realized it would be better to eat the little brother, while the big brother was tortured by the guilt and terror that he could do nothing; oh the guilt and hopelessness would make him so much sweeter. The little monster made eye contact with the big brother while he took a step towards the little brother. The little monster couldn't speak English, but he knew that his eyes would tell the big brother exactly what he meant to do. The big brother started crying and screaming and kicking again, fighting like a hero. He felt like he would do anything to rescue his "cry baby" little brother, but... it was useless. The little brother started shivering like he was having a seizure. The little monster opened his mouth bigger and finally the teeth started to part. By now his teeth were so big that for his mouth to open it was like he was unhinging his jaw. He almost looked like an old-fashioned bear trap, just with much longer teeth. The monster was right there now, teeth and jaws all open. The big brother screamed, the little brother cried, the monster squealed, the Widow's Tree shuddered, the breeze picked up into a strong gust of wind and...

... blew out the lantern.

Good Dog

Good Dog

This story is mostly the firsthand account of the boy in it. We left out the gore for your benefit, but we could not leave out the danger and tragedy.

Jacob got Max as an adorable German shepherd puppy, a little puffball of energy. But Max was such an unusual dog for behavior. Some dog breeds and certain personality types are easier to train than others. But Max was a phenomenon. His family knew he was a really good dog; he seemed to learn tricks and commands like a genius. Though Jacob didn't realize how unusual Max was until many years later when he got more experience with dogs, he was always super proud. Frankly, I want to be proud for him. But it just makes it that much harder to accept... what Max did to people.

Max never barked or growled at the wrong people or for a silly reason. You could give Max food and take it right back and he wouldn't so much as nip for it. You could take a piece of meat right out of his mouth and he wouldn't even make a little snarl. That's rare. You have to wonder, with a dog that unusual, friendly and loyal and sensible, did some kind of dog demon take over his soul for what he did?

One day Jacob got in trouble with his dad before school. Jacob's dad yelled at him harshly and grounded him. Jacob left for school furious and crying. He walked to school with his neighbor. Jacob rode back from school with his mom. She entered the house first. Jacob had forgotten about his dad yelling at him. His brain was filled up with school things. He walked up to the door without any bad feelings. So when he heard his mother scream the worst scream he ever heard in his life, he had no way of knowing.

And what was in that house... I can never rewrite, even in a book that promises to be disturbing. But Jacob did not have a father anymore and the reminders splattered around the walls could never be cleaned enough.

His mother ran into the house, but fainted while she was running and fell face-flat on the bloody floor. Max ran to Jacob to greet him, all licks and wagging tail. Every lick made ice go down Jacob's spine and every wag made the room spin. Max, the best dog, the very best dog in the whole world... couldn't possibly... Jacob was barely able to call 911 before he fell unconscious himself. Max watched over him and kept whimpering and trying to lick him awake.

Jacob and his mom both woke up with paramedics and police and everything everywhere. The police didn't do anything with Max because Max was being perfectly safe and friendly when they came. But when the police were sure that Max was the killer, they told Jacob's mom that they would call animal control to come and get the dog. Well either the police forgot or animal control forgot because when Jacob and his mom got home from their short stay at the hospital, Max was still there. It's just not right. If you come home to a regular murderer, you might know exactly what to do, like run away, call 911. But when the murderer is your loving and loyal dog, you don't know what to do. Not knowing what to do made everything hard. It made it hard for Jacob's mother to breathe. But she waited patiently and tried to hide her breathing problems for Jacob's sake.

Jacob's mom thought maybe the delay was about warrants or paperwork. It was hard for her. She LOVED Max. She loved Max almost as much as she loved Jacob, he had been part of the family for years and he was such a good dog. But living with a murderer, a furry, cuddly, loyal murderer, will make you insane. So after waiting a couple days, she knew she had to call animal control herself and make them take Max away. She waited until Jacob left for school. She didn't want to upset him. But Jacob forgot his homework. He came back into the house and heard her talking to animal control. Jacob already understood that Max had to go; the smell of fresh paint on the wall and new carpet on the floor reminded him why Max had to go. Jacob understood... and yet he didn't. He wasn't old and mature enough to emotionally cope with it. Maybe no one would be. Jacob needed his loyal dog more now that he didn't have a father. It's crazy, but it's crazy while being true human psychology. Jacob cried. He cried very hard. And Max saw him cry. Jacob tried to be brave and good and left to school, still crying though.

Jacob didn't make it to school. He couldn't tell the teacher THIS problem. Instead he hid in a neighbor's treehouse for hours. When Jacob went home... he was all alone... except for Max... and his mom's dead body. And Max wouldn't let Jacob leave anymore.

Now Jacob's life was completely off the rails. No matter how long Jacob waited, Max guarded all the doors when Jacob went near them. If Jacob tried to use a phone, Max... Max the once perfect dog... would snap at his hands like a beast from hell. Jacob couldn't ever leave the house. Max would sneak out of the house himself at strange times. He would drag back food like bags of bread or a cat he had killed. Jacob had to learn to live off of such food. After a while the electricity was cut off because nobody paid the bill. Jacob couldn't watch TV. He got used to cold showers. He started doing his school books because there was nothing else to do. He could still play with Max, except that it's hard to play with your dog around the blood stains he made. Jacob's school books got old and Max brought home more books. Max understood too much for a real dog, but Jacob couldn't understand Max.

Jacob was a prisoner to his own "good dog" for years. After 12 years of this, Jacob was more than an adult and Max started to show his age. Max would sit down kind of sideways. It took him an extra wiggle to stand back up. Jacob began to wonder if Max needed medicine. That's right, after 12 years of imprisonment and two murders, Jacob didn't think about Max's weakness as a chance to escape; he just worried if Max was okay. He knew Max wouldn't let him out for help, though. Jacob knew that he would have to escape. Jacob decided to escape from Max so that he could get Max a doctor or something.

Jacob decided to trap Max in the backyard. The backyard and the front yard had a side path connecting them. There was a short gate they had put in when Max was a puppy, specifically for keeping him in the backyard. Jacob would have to close that without Max noticing. Then he would have to lure Max into the backyard and get back into the house without him. This would be hard because Max usually walked right by Jacob's side.

Jacob spent all afternoon in the backyard, waiting for Max to fall asleep. Max finally went to asleep and Jacob crept over as quietly as he could. He moved as slowly as possible closing the gate. It was never used; he didn't know if it would be full of creaks and scrapes. There were no creaks, but there was a dull scrape of the wood against concrete. It wasn't loud, but every tiny sound made Jacob's hair stand on the back of his neck. He was still terrified of Max catching him doing something. The clasp was sticking. It wouldn't close right because it didn't line up right anymore. Jacob had to lift the gate into alignment and hold the clasp so that it wouldn't fall closed with a metal tink.

He did it. He turned around expecting to see Max watching him, gray muzzled, but still deadly. But Max seemed to still be asleep. He seemed undisturbed. Jacob tried slipping into the house already, but as soon as the sliding glass door moved, Max got up and ran over.

Jacob started to panic and sweat. He was afraid that Max would smell his betrayal. Dogs smell weird things, like fear and cancer. But Jacob still had to try. Jacob got a piece of food and threw it far into the backyard. That didn't work on Max. Max was never an idiot for food like other dogs, and besides Max could get his own food. Jacob wasn't thinking clearly. This was a silly, panicky idea. Who knows what these mistakes could cause? Jacob ordered Max to fetch the food, certain that his trembling voice would reveal his dishonest intent. But Max immediately obeyed. Jacob slammed the sliding door shut. And locked it for good measure. Max spun on him, barking ferociously. All the age was gone from Max. He sprang around like a 2-year-old dog, fresh, ready to tear a grizzly bear to shreds. The demon that hid in the corner of Max's soul must have come out and filled all his muscles. It filled his eyes. But worse it filled his teeth, dripping wet and ten times bigger than usual. Jacob tried to sprint to the front door, but he was clumsy now too, so he kept hitting corners of shelves and tables and doorways. He ran into so many things it was almost like he ran into things that weren't there. When he got to the front door he looked to the back door. Max wasn't there barking anymore. Jacob knew that Max had run for the side path already. Jacob ran out the front door. He didn't pause to close it. Max, old Max, who was starting to sit funny and take naps all day, had been able to jump over the side fence. Jacob sprinted for the front fence, fortunately there were no tables to run into, but he had to climb the front fence without Max getting him. He jumped and started climbing. Max bit his pants. Jacob was grateful and surprised that Max didn't just bite through his whole leg. Max was pulling hard, but Jacob had got enough of his weight over the fence that he was able to kind fall over it, while Max got caught against the fence and Jacob's pants tore out of his mouth. Jacob got up and started running again, slower because he was already winded. He hadn't run for 12 years. The front fence was higher than the side fence. Maybe Max wouldn't clear it. Max backed up. He didn't bark anymore. The demon would give no more warnings, now it was time for punishment. Max sprinted, he leapt. Max did clear the fence, but his feet caught when he did it and he landed badly. Max was hurt; his knees were scraped deep, but he got up right away and chased Jacob. Max was injured, but Jacob was clumsy and panicky, and he was only a human, not a dog with the soul of a demon. Max caught up to Jacob fast.

Jacob looked like a lunatic to other people, running down the street in ragged clothes, screaming. And his screaming was garbled and didn't make sense because of years of not talking to people. High school kids walking home from school stayed away from him instead of helping. No one even reached for their phone when they saw Max reach Jacob and yank him down to the ground in the middle of the street. Finally, by fate, a driver accidentally hit Max without hitting Jacob. People started to get the guts to get closer and see what was happening.

Multiple 911 calls came in reporting a drug addict and a wolf. When the police arrived, Max was on his feet again and slowly but stubbornly dragging Jacob back to the house. Jacob was unconscious and everyone else was afraid to stop Max.

The police officer pulled his gun out to shoot Max. But Max, who never saw a gun fired in his life, seemed to understand the gun. Supernatural Max. He let go of Jacob, he backed off. He went friendly. The police officer lowered the gun, but it was still a standoff. Max couldn't take Jacob back without getting shot. The officer couldn't go save Jacob without risking getting bitten. Max stared at the officer a long time. Another police car came up. Max, the once perfect dog, ran away. The officer brought his gun up, but couldn't take a safe shot. Max got away.

They say that Jacob became a nighttime dog catcher. They say that he drifts from town to town following rumors. He comes out late at night and only talks about one thing, how he used to have this "good dog" and… "Have you seen him?"

Grandson

Grandson

This one was sent in from a police officer fan. This case had raised alot of eyebrows in his office.

The old woman got a call very late at night. The voice said, "Grandma, it's me, your grandson. I'm having an emergency. I need you to send me money right away!"

Grandma was so confused; she was afraid to say it to him, but she had only had one grandson, Marcus, and she thought he was dead.

"I know you're surprised to hear from me, Grandma, but this is an emergency. I need your help right away!"

So she had to help him. He gave her a place to wire money to. It was in Brazil. Grandma got her things together and went to wire the money right away. While she was driving she was trying to understand. But it was hard. This was all so sudden. And she was old; she couldn't remember anything and got confused by everything anyway. He must have been kidnapped in Brazil. She couldn't say if that made sense or not. So she just went on with it. Her poor little grandbaby.

The next morning she called and told her daughter. Her daughter yelled at her, "Grandma, how can you be so naïve!? That was a scam! They took advantage of you. You need that money!"

Grandma was so embarrassed when she saw her daughter. Her daughter told her all about the scam where young men call old ladies and pretend to be a grandchild. She was so easy to trick. But still, it really sounded like Marcus.

"Marcus didn't disappear in South America, Grandma. He was killed in the U.S. by a texting driver. He's not going to show up in some foreign country. I'm so sorry."

Grandma went home and cried by herself for being so stupid and helpless. Also, all this made her miss Marcus again.

That night she got another call. The voice said he was her grandson and he still needed money, more money, at a different location in Brazil. Grandma scolded that young man for running scams on elderly women, even though his voice sounded exactly like Marcus. Exactly. So then the voice started to prove that he was her grandson. He said the hospital where he was born, his hometown, and his mother's name. Grandma didn't understand, but she had to help him. This time it wasn't just her extra savings, she was going to miss her rent payment. But she had to help her poor little grandbaby; Grandma can't say no.

This time her daughter just cried, no screaming.

"Grandma, how could you? They do that. They find personal information. Anyone can find this online. He tricked you... again. Oh Grandma, we have to get you some money now. But we have to close your accounts so you can't do this again.

"But his voice, it was exactly little Marcus's voice."

"I don't know, Grandma, but he's dead, my little Marckie is dead and we both saw it with our own eyes. He's buried, Grandma, and he's gone and this is killing me."

Grandma could only apologize again and again. But she couldn't help repeating how much the voice was the same. But it made her daughter cry so much that she had to stop saying it.

They closed Grandma's accounts, came up with money for her rent, and took her home. Grandma had dreams that night. Then she realized they weren't dreams. She was still awake, lying in bed, seeing old memories of Marcus replay over and over again, alot like dreams.

The phone rang. It startled her even though she knew exactly what it was. She ignored it and rolled over and felt heartbroken and alone. But the phone kept ringing. It would hit the maximum number of rings, stop, and ring again. She answered. What could someone in Brazil do to her anyway? And this little scammer, he was somebody's grandbaby. He needed help too.

She told the voice that she couldn't give him money. The voice said he didn't need money now. He just needed to be picked up from the airport. He escaped Brazil, made it to America, and needed someone to pick him up. Grandma told the young man that he wasn't really her grandson. But the young man told her a story from his childhood. It was one of the memories she had just been replaying all alone. She thought it was anyway. It was a time when she snuck him some candy so his mom wouldn't know. This couldn't be looked up on the Internet. And Marcus's voice was the voice on the phone. And he wasn't asking for money anyway. Grandma got her things. She left a note on the kitchen counter and took Grandpa's old pistol. She went to pick up her dead grandson.

Nobody saw or even heard what happened at the airport. It was so late at night. But someone in the early morning found the bodies. There was Grandma with strangle marks on her neck and there was a young man, shot dead. They called Grandma's daughter to identify the old woman's body. They also had the daughter check the young man's body. The daughter fainted. She said that the body looked exactly like Marcus would have... if he grew up.

It doesn't end there.

When the daughter went to clean Grandma's things out of the house, the phone started ringing. She tried to ignore it and keep working, but it wouldn't stop. Finally she thought maybe the police were calling about something important on this line. When she picked up, someone was asking for Grandma... in Marcus's voice. When she tried saying "Marcus" the phone hung up. But it rings again and again, a couple times a night, asking for Grandma. The daughter was so traumatized that she had Marcus's body exhumed, against everyone's advice, just so she could check it. His little remains are there in the coffin. Now Grandma's remains are in her coffin. But the phone still rings asking for Grandma to send money, telling stories from the life of a boy and his family. The house was sold. The phone line was ordered shut off by the police, but whenever management changes, and someone new at the phone company doesn't know, they reassign the phone number... and the calls come again. Missing person after missing person... for two decades and counting.

Hotel

This story was told to me orally by an old childhood friend. (You start getting all kinds of stuff you never heard before when you let people know you have a project like this.) I tried to write it down as close to word-for-word as possible, but I probably messed up some.

"I went on a weekend trip to an out-of-the way island country. I arrived Friday night at my hotel. The first thing I did was to open up my bag and put out my good luck travel bear. It's a little porcelain clown bear, pretty awful looking by most people's standards, but I thought it was great. I bought it the first time I went to another country as a kid and I decided it was good luck. Whenever I brought it with me I never had any traveler's problems: no scams, no pickpockets, no diarrhea, no losing things. It just felt like it really worked. My fiancé was with me too. When she got in the room she just dropped her luggage, took a short look at our view, and crashed on the bed. I set my shaving things on the bathroom counter. I organized my clothes in the closet. I'm certain I did. I always do.

When my fiancé and I went out the next day we had a great time, the food, the history. We saw everything. Everybody spoke English well so it was really easy to get around and explore and ask questions. We bought the coolest knickknacks. We came back late and fell straight asleep. In the morning I realized that my good luck bear was missing. The hotel we were staying at was super small, just a dozen rooms. I went to the lady at the desk, who I think was also the owner, and as carefully and politely as I could, accused the cleaning lady of taking my little clown bear. She said she cleaned our room herself that day because the cleaning lady was off. I didn't want to accuse her, so I dropped it.

My fiancé and I went out all day again Sunday. My fiancé wanted to shop for clothes and handbags so I spent alot of time people-watching on my own. I even got to mixing with the locals. The things I ate and drank were amazing and sometimes gross. I caught a fish with some youngsters on the dock. I let a couple brothers take it home, though. It was just crazy, random fun.

I woke up Monday, our last day of the little trip. My girlfriend had gone out already. Then when I went to shave, all my shaving stuff was gone. I went to talk with the hotel lady and didn't get anywhere. She kept talking me in circles, but not like in an evasive way, just really in a confusing way. She was so interesting and unique, all the locals were so fascinating, it just made me forget everything. It was such a great trip, it was worth losing some things, y'know?

So I went out on the streets again. Lots of people were "missing". Sunday had had fewer people out than Saturday, but not like this. Probably more locals come out for the tourists on weekends. They have regular gigs to do the rest of the week. The people I did come across couldn't speak much English. Their sentences were really broken and hard to follow. They were less talkative and animated too. I guess if you're busy with your normal life you don't have time for tourists. I was still so curious about the culture, though. Now I wanted to see their real culture when they're not pandering to tourists. But then I found a porcelain clown bear at a market stall, exactly like mine. I don't know if it was my own bear being sold to me, but it could have been. I went ahead and bought it, feeling both anxious and comforted. I guess I was just tired of the vacation already.

I didn't see my girlfriend all that day until back at the hotel. She wanted to stay an extra day so we spent the evening arranging the hotel and flights. Atleast I had my good luck bear back. But my sleep was kind of restless. I kept feeling like the bed was empty. When I woke up the next day my girlfriend's things weren't even in the room. All of my clothes were set up nicely in the closet, but my luggage case was missing, and still my shaving kit and the bear. I mean the bear was missing again. I started to feel very vulnerable. I went to talk to the hotel lady. I had to wait a long time for her to answer the bell. I was getting suspicious of her. She said my girlfriend went out early and would meet me. Who knows where? I didn't get anywhere with finding out where my missing things were, but she was still really friendly with me and I wanted to trust her. I wanted to be friends with the quirky hotel lady. I think I was starting to feel all alone, too.

I went out, but no one spoke English at all. I mean at all. I just people-watched. I met my girlfriend for dinner. It was really hard to talk to her. We'd been having relationship trouble lately. I think she wanted to break up. How can something not be wrong when she books a different hotel room for our vacation?

When I woke up Wednesday it was really cold for this place. Half my clothes and stuff were gone, but I didn't even care. I was just depressed and miserable. I wanted to go cuss out somebody. When I looked outside it was all foggy and I could only see a couple of people and cars moving around so I decided not to go out until the weather was better. I checked my phone and social media and stuff. I normally never do that kind of thing on vacation, but I wasn't having my regular vacation, so why not? Besides, I needed to hear from a friend.

I wished I had invited my girlfriend along on the trip even if we were having problems. Nobody was hardly posting on social media, it was mostly old stuff and repeat shares. I noticed half of my friends were gone on all my accounts. I didn't have the heart to look into it then. I knew it had to be a glitch, but I just couldn't deal with it, not in that mental condition. I went down a couple times to talk to the hotel lady, but she was only there once. It felt really good to talk to someone. That night I even tried to call my mom, but my mom's contact number was missing from my phone. I shook with a huge chill that went down my whole spine. Was this some elaborate scam on tourists. Whatever, such a silly thought, like someone was stealing my contacts now? Still, so hard to beat the loneliness.

On Thursday the fog was heavy, like nothing I've ever seen, I couldn't see a soul outside. I was down to my last pair of pants and shirt, but whatever. My phone was gone and the hotel lady couldn't tell me anything about it, but I didn't care. I was just waiting for my flight home. How long had I been here? Why did I come on this vacation all alone? Why didn't I bring my phone? I didn't want my phone anyway, it seemed like I'd been losing friends lately. I stayed in my room to watch TV. There was nothing in English, in fact most of the stations were snow. Only one station came in clearly and it was all soap operas in the native language. I don't even know what language. It sounded Spanish, but it wasn't. But I left it on all day just to hear people's voices.

When I woke up, it was night. I tried to step outside. It was frighteningly dark as if someone had been stealing the streetlights or the stars or both, but atleast that fog was gone. But as soon as I stepped into the street I heard sirens. I couldn't hear where they were coming from so I went straight back in the hotel. I ran through the hotel. I didn't hear any TVs on. I didn't hear anyone talking or moving. I knocked on doors, but doors didn't open. I checked the front desk. I looked at the list. No other rooms were booked. The sign on the desk said, "Back in 15." I went outside again, but the sirens were still going. I couldn't see their flashing lights, I couldn't see anybody. I could just hear the sirens.

I slept like I was on rocks and nails. In the morning I had nothing. I had to go out in the hotel pajamas. The hotel was in bad disrepair. Paint and plaster were falling off. Exposed wood was rotting. Strange that this hotel would even provide pajamas. Every time I rang the front desk bell, the hotel lady said, "Coming!" but she never came out. And the voice always came from a different place. I tried stepping outside in that terrible fog. I could swear I saw my ex-girlfriend going down the street and into the fog. I couldn't believe she happened to be on a trip here too. I ran after her to catch her, but... but.

For hours I would barely see a face, one of the fishing boys, a market person, even just a cat. But everyone I tried to reach just... became the fog. I kept getting the feeling that stray dogs were following me. Hungry dogs. But I saw nothing. My legs got exhausted from searching. If I had heard sirens I would have ran to them. I wanted to call 911, but my phone... missing. I found churches-- empty, and docks-- no boats, and parking lots-- no cars. At some corner cafe I saw one meal, but no one eating it, no one serving it, and while I was hungry, somehow it didn't seem safe to eat. I just stared at it. In my mind I was eating it; I was talking to a waiter. But I couldn't eat it for real and just stood back for my stomach to eat itself, while my brain kept trying to talk to itself... with no one answering.

The hotel was abandoned and condemned, but I didn't have anywhere else to sleep so I snuck inside and curled up on some old mattresses with some mildewy sheets that made me sneeze all night.

When I woke up the next day, everything was back. My bear, my shaving kit, my luggage, even my fiancé's things. But no people were there. Not my fiancé, not the hotel lady, no one else in the hotel. Outside all the markets were up, products laid out. There were cars, and boats, and dishes for dog or cat food, but no living thing was there, not even a bird. My phone was back, but I couldn't call anyone. No one picked up. No one texted back. No one posted. I would have eaten my own hand for someone to talk to. I would've talked to the people I hate most in the world. I just sat in the middle of the street holding myself and rocking on the ground. Rocking and screaming and crying and praying that a car would come along and hit me... right in the face. In death I could talk to somebody, other dead people, or atleast the devils.

My alarm went off, back at home, in bed, time to go to work. It was all a dream. It was all a dream except it wasn't. I wake up in that hotel. I relive the nightmare. I try different things to break the curse. I will do anything to keep the loneliness from coming to me. The suicidal thoughts... I didn't want to mention the suicidal thoughts because it would worry you. I've tried learning the language, I tried breaking the good luck bear. I even decided once to kill the hotel lady and search her rooms for... secrets, stolen items, some kind of conspiracy with videos and audio recordings, I don't know. I'm never able to kill her anyway. I got a chance once to break into some of her rooms, but there was nothing special, no mystery stash of stolen goods or bizarre film revealing... anything.

Whenever I seem to lose a friend. Whenever someone even forgets to text me back, I wake up in that hotel. And the loneliness cannot be fought. You can't fight back against the absence of monsters. You can't call the no-police to protect you from the no-stray dogs. You can't even call your mom. The loneliness is inside you, in a way that you can't cut out. You would. You'd take a saw to your own brain if you felt like I've felt. You better watch out.

Please don't leave me right now. Stay with me until I have someone to go with. Or the hotel will be waiting for me."

Plane Crash
Survivor

Plane Crash Survivor

This story was put together from police reports and rumors, but the most incredible part of the story has been confirmed by incontrovertible evidence; we have an actual sample of animal-like fur with human DNA.

They believe the person in question was James T. Hort, a wealthy man whose plane matches the wreckage and who went missing at the right time. The wreckage was found in the mountains by hikers. Fortunately for the hikers, they didn't attempt to follow any trail and find survivors. The police explored the wreckage and found a severed human foot, apparently torn off in the crash. They investigated all the local hospitals to see if a one-footed survivor had turned up. Unfortunately, no one had seen such a man and that meant combing the woods to find him. It took two weeks to find the trail. It would have been best if they never found his trail at all.

The "trail" was animal carcasses that had limbs cut off, like only a human would do. But the cuts were bad as if done with scrap metal, like from plane wreckage. And the animals weren't killed with bullets or even arrows. They had trauma to the head and neck from some kind of crude weapons. So maybe you ask, "What's wrong with a lost person hunting to survive?" What's wrong is that these animals were all too fast and too strong to be killed by a human. People can't catch deer. Mature gentlemen don't strike down a bear. Something was terribly unnatural here and the investigating officers didn't ignore the warning signs. They got all the searchers armed and on the lookout for something very dangerous and out of the ordinary.

When they followed trails all over the mountainside they found that paths all gathered to the same place, the opening of a cave, Mr. Hort's apparent temporary home.

There can be only one even remotely scientific explanation for what happened to James. Adrenaline is a powerful thing. It makes you incredibly strong and tough, but it also puts huge stress on your body. Stress and different things have certain effects on you, even effects on your DNA. You see there's something called epigenetics. Proven science has shown that there are parts of your DNA that are never "expressed" unless certain conditions are met. The extreme event that Mr. Hort survived may have triggered certain abnormal gene expression. The adrenaline may have pushed his muscles so hard and so long past their normal limits that he became permanently stronger... far stronger. Maybe the intense cold, or something about stress and epigenetics made him grow animal-like fur; the fur mentioned in the beginning. It has canine structure and color banding, but the DNA matches pure human; more perfectly, it matches the DNA of the severed foot in the plane. The event may even have started changing his bone structure, making him look less human, and move differently. And that missing foot didn't slow him down much. Whether he was able to outrun a deer or if he just learned to ambush them, he still had to be incredibly fast, faster than a deer's sprint or faster than a deer's reflexes or both.

Bigfoot rumors in that area started to incorporate a spike-foot attribute. They sometimes called him Spikefoot and claimed that he could run on steep, loose hillsides, with his spike foot regaining traction whenever his human foot slipped, like he was half mountain goat... and half mountain lion.

When the search officers gathered up to investigate the cave they were tense and serious. No one was treating this as a joke. If only they had more sense. They had plenty of guns, plenty of lights, and plenty of men, but they should've just not walked into that cave. They readied up, screamed and charged in like they were invading a drug lord's fortress. They thought they might scare this beast-man into cowering in a corner. What a mistake. This was nothing like a drug lord's fortress. And the survivor was like a beast, but not.

Their walkie-talkies were useless inside the cave; the signals couldn't go through the thick stone. And the cave was so deep and took so long to explore that the batteries started going dead on the lights. And the cave split into so many forks that the groups got smaller and smaller from all that splitting up. Soon they were just ones and twos. Besides, accidents happen. Some of the men didn't mean to separate, confused in the dark, climbing and crawling through a nature-made maze. They wanted to be careful, but they were lost, very tired, and confused. And being tired and confused makes you less smart. One mistake causes another until... well, in this case, until you die.

What really went wrong is all rumors and speculation: dead flashlights, sprained ankles, broken bones from unexpected pitfalls in the dark; screaming covering the approach of a deranged murderer, and panic gunfire shooting the friends. What good does the training do you if you have slippery palms, tripping feet, and sweat running down in your eyes so bad you're blinded from the sting of it? Even if your body were working, your mind is useless from fear.

Maybe you get mad and stressed when someone is screaming and hollering so loud you can't hear what's moving around you. But that anger probably changes into something much worse when you hear that screaming go dead silent. What if you get a knife out so you can fight that monster without shooting your friends, but that knife just ends up in your own neck because you can't see the Spikefoot coming? What if it still hasn't come for you, but you fell in a dark pit and your leg bone busted through your muscle and skin? And you don't know if you're going to slowly bleed to death or get eaten by the psycho?

No one can say how the rangers died because no one who went in that cave ever come out. Only two rangers came away, the two who waited by the entrance and had the good, cowardly sense not to run in and try to save anyone. They reported what they heard happen and made up the rest.

It was probably like killing babies for the plane crash survivor. In the darkness Hort picked all the rangers off. No one knows why. Maybe part of the mutation was that he became a homicidal maniac. Or maybe he was afraid of them, like any animal protecting its home. Or maybe he was just really, really hungry. At any rate, Hort's murders would have to go unpunished. Some people say he ate all the victims. Some people say he impaled them all on stakes around his cave as a warning never to bother him again. And some people say he did both. No one will ever go back to the spot to find out. The government didn't go back for bodies. They didn't even try to find survivors. But maybe that doesn't matter. The legend of Spikefoot is spreading. Maybe it's because his territory is spreading too. Maybe he's not there anymore. Maybe he's living by you.

Raluca
Loveridge

Raluca Loveridge: The Demon Witch

When you talk about witchcraft in the modern era, many women will tell you that there are no such things as demon witches. "Witches were women who worshipped pagan goddesses. For that they were hated by the patriarchal church. Any so-called demonic witches are just fakes looking for attention." However, if you find the right person, they will tell you that demonic witches are very real, "They believe in seeking the powers of devils and demons. Pagans only claim that the witch hunts targeted them so they can get glory for being martyrs." Our research of many documents, public and private, from the 1600s, revealed some disturbing truths: 1) demonic witchcraft is a rare, but fervently followed religious practice, 2) the witch trials targeted anyone who caused concern: demonic witches, pagans, sometimes Christians, mostly women, but some men and even children, and 3) one demonic witch earned the wrath of society; she caused death and disease in acts of terror that could hardly be accomplished by natural means. This is the story, taken from her own words, public news, and court documents, of Raluca Loveridge, the Demon Witch.

Raluca came to America knowing that the promise of religious freedom didn't apply to her. She knew that no one could accept demon worshippers. But she did come for space to practice. The Old World had become wary of witches. In

America, in the wild lands, she could practice unbothered. She could build her skills and her demonic bonds. And by the time anyone discovered her frightening practices, she would be too powerful to stop. That was her plan anyway. And reality very nearly turned out like her plan.

Loveridge often wore black. But it's not as you imagine. Every color was something of a spell. They all had a different focus. And certain combinations could have very different meanings. Black was tied with death, but black alone was for clean death, pure death. Black with red was for a bloody, bloody death. Black and yellow was for a diseased death. Now red alone was for blood, but it often wasn't to shed blood. If someone was weak and pale, red, blood magic would restore them. So you see, red could be part of a healing spell or a brutal killing spell. It can be quite simple, but some of the combinations get quite complicated and it's very disturbing to see Raluca calmly recording into her diary, like a scientist, the effects of her clothing colors on the health and lives of other human beings.

One reason she needed isolation was these clothes. She wore fine velvets, silks, and the best cottons. No one who wasn't royal dressed like this, certainly not in the American wilds. But fine clothes make fine magics. And fine clothes and fine magics cost money. What were her resources?

Slaves such as...

animal...

human...

and demon.

The very first slaves were brought to America in 1619. It took a long time for slaves to become central to the economy, but by the time Loveridge arrived in 1658 slaves were known enough that she could send any black man to do almost anything and no one would question it.

Raluca could also command animals like birds, squirrels, and raccoons to steal rings and purses and such. She also could command wolves to attack and wasps to swarm and sting. No animal was too intelligent or too unintelligent to fail her commands. And in case you experience strange things yourself, beware anyone during an animal attack who looks at you instead of the attacking animal. That is how the spell works. Normal humans watch the animal because of fear. The witches watch the victim... to do the spell.

The most impressive and most dangerous of her slaves were demons. Of course, all demonic witches draw power from a demon familiar, but Raluca Loveridge boasted that her skill and reputation became so great that she commanded multiple demons, and the demons supposedly called on her to ask for favors. Sure, demons had great powers beyond that of humans, but Raluca had great knowledge of the human world; demons can be shockingly ignorant. It's one thing to believe Raluca's diaries about her powers, but seeing the news reports of things that happened around Raluca Loveridge is another. Evil will never mean the same thing to you if you read further on.

In 1690, in a dense and rotten woods of Middlesex, Massachusetts, Raluca Loveridge was approximately fifty years old and probably more powerful than any other witch ever. She had been poisoning or butchering people who wandered through or tried to settle in her woods. Still, people were encroaching. All the local snakes were complaining to her about how often they saw humans in the woods. She was packing up and preparing to move when she decided to try one more experiment in her old woods.

American settlers had great get-togethers when big work needed doing. They invited everyone nearby to help raise a barn or some such thing and then celebrated at night with music and food in reward for their neighbors' work. Instead of Raluca's normal practice of poisoning or hacking up one or two poor lost souls in her woods, Loveridge realized she might summon a demon and kill a whole party of families, a deliberate tactic to terrify anyone else from coming near her woods. Sure, it would attract attention too, maybe cause a war, but she could atleast try. And if the war were too much for her, she could flee later.

But to kill a whole party she should summon a very strong demon, no tiny, unknown forked-tail. How strong? Why not experiment with how high up the demon hierarchy she could go? Raluca Loveridge, the most powerful demon witch in known history, decided to summon Beelzebub, second only to Satan himself, to kill a party of innocent farmers and homesteaders, just to see if she could do it. And Beelzebub himself did answer the call, compelled by her magic, and serving *her* will.

Everyone, all the men, women, and children at the barn party were slaughtered. Loveridge spent the night dancing in glee. Local records say an Indian raiding party killed everyone at that farmhouse. We know this wouldn't be true because it is very out of the ordinary that the records didn't identify a particular tribe. They probably couldn't identify a particular tribe because there weren't really any signs of any Indian tribes.

Raluca showed disappointment about that news article in her journal. She wanted the credit for the massacre, but maybe this was better for her. She wasn't quite ready for all-out war. Terror and confusion might be better than deaths blamed on a single witch. She started spying more and playing at political affairs. She relied heavily on love spells. Her favorite, the strongest, required using no magic on the victim before they kiss you. She would charm important men from the towns, make them fall for her, and once they kissed her... mm, she could command them to do anything. She used them for spying, controlling the commoners, and playing them to kill each other in duels like puppets.

Loveridge hated men, mentioned it in her diaries all the time, but never said why. She was disgusted by their kiss, but relished in her ultimate power over them. Under her home were found the remnants of 38 skeletons. Most of these were not properly stored by the county, but a few skeletons that were saved have been recently analyzed. Some of the supposedly single skeletons actually have mixed bones from two or three men. Raluca's diary implies more than fifty men should be buried. Women were not targeted for mind-control or death, except in Raluca's massacres. Apparently Raluca preferred to punish women with disfigurement. One of her favorites was a wasp she had bred or magically altered to cause permanent scarring with its sting. Raluca couldn't mind-control children. But she would kill them and skin them and make manikins that looked and acted like real kids. Kids could fit places adults couldn't and walk into buildings that animals couldn't. The manikins could be made to attack people and the people who fought back found these "children" to be skins stuffed with straw. This last bit of evil was too much. Murdered children was not something the people could pretend wasn't really a problem.

People were already long suspicious of Loveridge. Finally suspicion and hate outweighed the proud American value of proper justice and fair procedure. The people of the nearest town decided to arrest her without evidence. Raluca let them. But what the deputies didn't know was that she had summoned multiple hives of wasps to follow her and wait under the eaves of the courthouse. When the town put her on "trial" and accused her of witchcraft, she summoned in thousands of wasps to sting everyone in the building. She laughed as she walked free. Some people died from the hysteria. Others died from the horrible medical treatments of the era. Many died from just so many stings. And all those that survived knew that Raluca was a true demon witch.

Loveridge started her war. She began to summon the biblical plagues on the nearby towns, locusts destroying the crops and starving families, water turning to blood and people dying of thirst. And every time she brought a plague, she summoned a different high-ranking demon to deliver it. All answered her powers: war generals like Astaroth and Agaliarept, and unholy princes such as Belphegor and Mammon. She bragged that the demon world had begun to both idolize and fear her. But at the peak of her vanity she ordered Beelzebub to walk into a church during the sermon and curse the pastor. Beelzebub did it, but it went badly for him. The whole congregation stared in horror as the massive demon walked into their church, pointed a strong and hideous finger at the minister, bellowed in some underworld tongue, and caused the preacher to burst out in blisters and sores. But Beelzebub had to escape as proudly as he could, for the holy wrath of the sacred church burned his skin and caused it to erupt in blisters and burns himself. Raluca had made a grave mistake in abusing her power on Beelzebub.

The townspeople appealed to the state for militia aid. More than 100 men with guns went to shoot Raluca Loveridge, her house, and every cursed animal in that woods. The people and that militia got very lucky. A hundred guns is a weak challenge to the legion of demons such as Loveridge could normally have summoned. Mother nature, Loveridge's past mistakes, and maybe the colonialists' God too, were on their side because a wildfire rose up behind Raluca's house and demons have to avoid uncontrolled fire. Raluca's spells hissed and fizzled as she failed to summon a demonic legion. Some pagan historians claim that pagan witches communed with nature and asked for that fire. At any rate, Raluca could not get demon aid. Her animals couldn't fight a hundred guns and they had to flee from fire too. Loveridge had to run herself. Several members of the militia saw a black deer narrowly escaping the fire when suddenly a demon appeared out of nowhere and seized the deer high into the air. Beelzebub, full of hate for the witch who enslaved him, who abused him, burned him and embarrassed him, came to kill Raluca for revenge. Several of the militia saw the black dear turn into Raluca in his giant hands. She screeched for mercy seconds before Beelzebub threw her deep into the fire.

Raluca Loveridge's remains were never given a Christian burial for obvious reasons. Her remains were stored with those of her unidentified victims and kept for hundreds of years with historical artifacts of the county. But Loveridge's remains have gone missing since. Like we said, demonic witches are rare but fervent. Most likely, someone out there still hopes to gain the power of the devils from under the earth. And maybe some hopeful demonic witch has stolen Raluca's infamous remains to serve as relics and spell channels. Maybe she will make an alliance with Beelzebub, and wage war on the innocent once again.

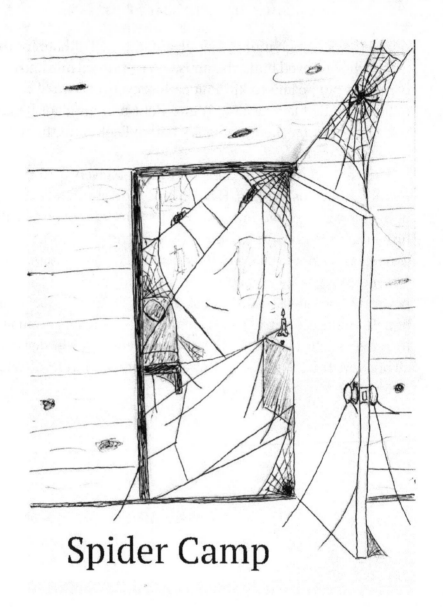

Spider Camp

Spider Camp

This was a hallucination one of my teachers had as a rare side-effect of prescription medication.

I was leading a troop of kids on a camping trip. They all got dropped off at the parking lot and then the parents left. I was the only adult with the kids. And the parking lot wasn't by the campground. We had to hike miles, up and down hill, with heavy backpacks. For some reason the kids weren't whining any. They were exhausted, but not whiny.

When we finally got to the campsite and cabins, something just wasn't right. We couldn't find a ranger. Everything was too quiet, even for a campsite. We tried going in the buildings; nothing was locked, but everything was so old. There was dust on everything and everything looked like it had been abandoned for years. I had to keep checking the name of the campsite to be sure I had the right place. It was the right place. We had a reservation here. It was the right name, anyway.

It was just starting to get dark. Everyone was really tired and getting drowsy. The bunk beds in the cabins were all ruined, broken wood with a few left-over, raggedy mattresses. The kids just started setting out their sleeping bags all over one cabin in between debris and broken wood. I started to notice some large, unusual spiders coming out and building webs. I tried not to worry about it; spiders don't care about people. I set out my own sleeping bag... I guess; I don't remember doing it. All I remember is waking up in my sleeping bag with the room all dark except for some bluish moonlight and somewhere a small flame. The weak orange light woke me up because I thought no one should leave a flame on while we sleep. It's not safe.

But when I became alert I saw more, and the truth is that the spiders were everywhere. They had built their webs all around, in every possible way. It was so you couldn't walk anywhere without ducking and walking sideways. And there were still spiders coming out and building new webs. It was like one of those movies with lasers guarding the treasure, except that the only treasure was getting out of the room. And the spiders were unnatural too. They were bold colors like royal blue or turquoise. And one type was shaped like big, long grasshoppers, only they weren't grasshoppers; they were spiders building webs. But I thought I saw some of them jump and fly a little bit to another spot. Everything was in this bluish moonlight with just a little, golden candlelight. I couldn't really see if the kids were okay; I could only see their sleeping bags so I hoped that they were all safe inside. I started trying to get past the spiderwebs without disturbing any spiders. They still didn't seem to want me, but I was sure that disturbing their webs would be a big mistake. At first I was still trying to get at the candle, but it was too difficult. Every step became blocked in by webs. It's like they were sewing me in. I just needed to get out of the room and away from the spiders' webs. I got a little desperate and panicky. I thought, maybe I could find a shovel outside and cut down the spiderwebs with that. I didn't even care if that was a good idea, it was just an excuse to get outside.

I finally made it out the back door, but there was a backyard like a house, not like a campground. I thought okay, I just need to get out of this yard too. Then I can think clearly. But when I tried to walk through the yard I realized there was dog poop in front of me. And more dog poop, and more poop. It felt like inside the house except instead of spiderwebs blocking the way, there was nowhere to step except in dog poop, all fresh dog poop. I was trying to tip-toe towards the back gate, going in between all the poop when suddenly I heard a growl. I didn't look back; I just imagined some red-eyed Doberman like a half-demon dog coming to get me. I started sprinting to the gate just stepping in all the fresh poop like it didn't matter; I needed to save my life. I pulled open the gate and on the other side a spider had filled up the whole frame with a big web... and I could see the spider resting right in the middle of it. I ran through it all, slamming the gate and then doing the crazy spider dance to try to get the spider off of me. I wanted to get it off me before it bit me. I never found the spider, but nothing was biting me either. "Not yet," I thought.

I saw lights on in the ranger's office. I ignored the poop on my shoes and just went on like it's normal to have poop on your shoes. I hurried to the ranger's office. Inside were three very strange men. They all looked like old yogis or fakirs from India. They were small old, men with very dark brown, very withered skin. They only wore cloths wrapped around their underwear zone plus cloths wrapped on their heads. They were working at desks with stacks of paper like it was a government office.

The strange men said they were working on the ant problem for the city. Suddenly I remembered that while hiking up to camp we had seen some ants eating a dead anaconda or land eel or something on the trail. The men said that those were mind-controlling ants that could take over everything if not stopped. Immediately I ran out to save the kids in case the ants were heading for them. When I ran out I saw a trail of ants. I was going to jump wide over it, but they called to me to talk to them. They told me the truth. Yes, they were mind-controlling ants, but they didn't work for themselves; they weren't normally interested in controlling people. But they were working for the old men. The old men weren't really trying to get rid of the mind-controlling ants. The strange men were trying to use the ants to control the city, and then maybe more.

I looked all around, thinking about how to save myself and my kids. If I took the trail back, I had the risk of running into the full army of mind-controlling ants. Then, in one direction, I saw a big green hill going higher. At the top was a pretty house with a radio tower. Hopefully, we could all go there and radio for help. The gray dawn was turning bright. I ran to our cabin. All the spiders seemed to be in hiding again and the webs were gone. I still had poop all over my shoes. I still didn't care. I ran in and woke up all the kids. They started rolling their sleeping bags, but I told them to forget everything. We got out the door of the cabin started going up to the green hill.

I don't know what was going on, but that green hill was crazy. There were little bunnies dressed up in tuxedos and dresses and dancing with each other. It would have been cute if I weren't running from spiders and ants and an evil cabal of office clerks. When we got to the house, the bunnies were gone, but I had a terrible feeling that someone was following us. We went in the house and I had the kids lock the doors while I found the radio equipment. I never used that stuff before, but I'm pretty sure it just didn't work. I tried everything; I couldn't even get it to turn on. Yes, I remembered to check that it was plugged in. There was no way for us to radio. Going there was for nothing. We would have to walk downhill and take our chances avoiding the mind-controlling ants.

I looked down the hill and saw men coming towards us. Forget about dancing bunnies. Forget about ants. Now a band of men with butcher knives and cleavers were coming up the hill. Some of the kids were freaking out when the psychos banged on the doors. The kids wanted to break out of the windows to run away, but that wouldn't work because the maniacs were breaking in the windows already. Everywhere glass was shattering, kids shrieked while killers were screaming. I saw a spider drop down from a broken window frame. I couldn't believe the spiders were attacking now too! But it landed onto one of the men. The murder-man wailed like a baby and ran away. I turned and saw another murderer straight behind me with his knife already raised up and coming down. I put up my hands to block, but a spider I hadn't noticed flew off of me and straight onto his face. He dropped to the ground rolling and flailing. His face started immediately turning black. It was happening all over the house. These guys were trying to hack up my kids, but spiders were jumping out at these cleaver-wielding savages. I saw one guy fall to the ground paralyzed and ants started coming out of his ear. I shuddered to see the ants running towards me—what if the ants got me and made me kill my kids? I ordered all the kids to run out of the house. Instinctively, without me saying anything, the kids stooped to pick up any spiders nearby and put them on their shoulders, even the most scaredy-cat kids.

I felt sick to my stomach when I saw that some of the kids were all cut up with glass or blades. One boy had a terrible stab wound in his stomach. Many had gaping slashes in their arms—you could see the white bone under the gathered blood. We did first aid while we were moving, only tying shirts around the ones flowing blood. Just regular bleeding, bleeding that you would consider alot if it happened at school, we ignored.

I suddenly realized that I didn't know how many kids I was supposed to have so I couldn't count. I didn't remember seeing any dead kids back in the house. It felt too late to go back. I didn't want to have to tell any parent that I left their child behind. But I also couldn't risk what might happen if some of those ants got on us now.

We were making good time away from the house. Everything seemed safe until we saw a swarm of ants on the path... running at us. There were too many. We'd be surrounded in seconds. Before I could decide what to do, the grasshopper spiders went flying at the ants. The bigger fat-bodied spiders dropped down and lumbered in as fast as they could while the little jumpers sprang ahead. They all clashed in a miniature monster melee. Of course the spiders were much stronger, but the ants had so many numbers. I realized finally that the spiders hadn't built webs all over the cabin to trap us. The spiders were shielding us. But I couldn't stay to see what happened here. My kids wisely started running around the swarm and I had to follow.

I don't know if all the kids survived the camp because the hallucination ended. The day after that hallucination, I went back to my doctor and told him to never give me that medicine again. Apparently, hallucinations are a super unusual side-effect for that drug, but it happens to about 1 in 10,000 patients. I'm afraid of everything in that hallucination. I'm afraid of dog poop. I'm afraid of bunnies and ants. I'm afraid of pretty houses and green hills. For some reason I'm even afraid of spiders. I like spiders, but I'm still afraid.

The Gashadokuro

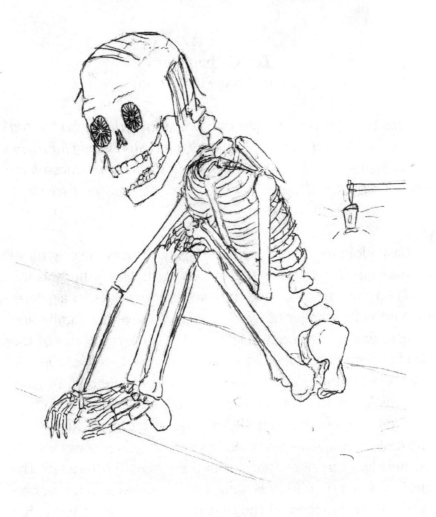

The Gashadokuro
(The Starved Skeleton)

This account comes from my own grandfather, who started telling me the stories when I was still a little too young for them. Many nights then, I would have to go to sleep curled uncomfortably as a tight ball, desperate not to let any body part stick out and tempt the gashadokuro.

Gashadokuros were born in Japan. It was just a naïve teenage girl who released this evil on earth. Her father was the lord of a small territory and they were under attack by a greater warlord with a larger army. Desperate to save her family and village, she used ancient magic to bring back the bones of the dead to fight. The spell didn't only raise up the old skeletons; it gave the bones power to unite into larger skeletons. You can imagine, eight-foot tall bone men easily destroyed even master samurai. The enemy army fled and never returned. Rumors of the castle being guarded by an undead army kept away would-be invaders for more than a hundred years. Fortunately the rival warlords didn't know what really happened. That underworld army disappeared the first night. The spirit energy that bound the skeletons could not be sustained and the bones all dropped to the ground as dead as ever.

The townspeople had to bury the scattered bones of loved ones again. They squirmed uncomfortably as they dug, thinking about the terrible way that their village had been saved, grumbling about the curse that would be brought on their land. Remember, it was the lord's daughter, a princess, who used that magic. Though her intent had been pure and she was noble of birth, no one would forgive her for doing something like that. She was put to death for using black magic. Her father was honor-bound to order the execution. That poor girl died. But the magic had still been done, and the bones had still learned something. They learned how to join together. Bones remember forever.

It takes great spirit energy to give life to dead bones. But there is often great energy in the suffering and misery of poor people. Generations later, when a greedy and reckless lord caused thousands of people to be starved to death, great spiritual pain spread all over the land. And while the bones were buried, the pain seeped through the soil and swirled and gathered into a great suffering hatred. And the strong spirit energy reached the old bones of the undead army. The energy "talked." The dark knowledge of the undead army passed on to the hateful and desperate bones of the starved. Then the bones of all the poor starved peasants climbed out of their graves in one night. They joined together into one. They became the first ever gashadokuro.

This bony colossus, taller than five houses, could wait invisible, hid inside the dimension of magic and death, while watching the dimension of living reality. And when some late-night wanderer came along the street... CHOMP!!! gashadokuro bit off his head. Desperate to feed its tortured appetite, it went on to gobble down bones and meat and guts all together like a human dumpling. The gashadokuro doesn't even mind the clothes.

A couple of lucky drunks who fell down when they should've had their heads chomped survived to tell others about the ringing. The only warning when a gashadokuro is nearby, since they become invisible until they strike, is a terrible ringing in your ears. If you duck from the first head chomp and run away, maybe you can survive with just very dirty underwear.

My grandfather met the gashadokuro when in the Korean War. (He hadn't learned the Japanese legends about them.) The bone magic had spread out of Japan. My grandfather helped it spread more, not on purpose of course, but by the worst luck.

He had been surrounded by the enemy. His unit had been caught in a crossfire from evening into the next morning. They tried to dig down in holes and hide. It worked... to slow their slaughter. But one by one the enemy found the right angle to see a hiding soldier and shoot them or mortar them. Sometime after the dawn, my grandfather realized he was probably the only one left alive and that he certainly had no chance of rescue there. All of the friendly soldiers he could see were horribly injured... or long dead from the night before. Admittedly he couldn't see many, they had all been dug down hiding and there was war fog everywhere anyway. Bullets didn't seem to be whizzing by his head, but he realized he wouldn't be able to hear bullets whizzing anyway because there was a strong ringing in his ears. He thought that it must be hearing damage from the huge firefight and explosions. But we know that wasn't really it, don't we? All of a sudden he saw a giant skeleton appear and bite the head off of his injured friend. The skeleton was crouched on the ground. It gobbled up his friend... and another. It didn't realize my grandpa was still alive and uninjured. And when it did see him staring back in terror, it disappeared. Actually it was rushing at him from the ghost dimension, but it didn't work. My grandfather was more terrified by the monster skeleton that eats people than getting shot to death. My grandpa got up to run and he dove over some other bodies, but he jumped in the most strange way; his feet ended up where his head ought to be so that when the gashadokuro came out to bite him, it bit off his feet instead.

My grandfather looked back in horror as the monster crunched on his feet. It gnawed the leather of his boots while his blood came out over the giant teeth. You can imagine what it's like to see your own blood coming out of a monster's mouth, so my grandfather didn't look anymore. He turned around and started crawling away, as fast as he could, over the bodies of his unit, his own friends and all. He didn't know how fast the gashadokuro could move. So he looked back to see if he was crawling fast enough. The gashadokuro was crawling on hands and knees behind him. With its great size it could easily overtake my grandfather, but it kept stopping to eat the other bodies, always keeping its glowing eyes on my grandfather.

My grandfather said that when the gashadokuro swallows, you can't see the chewed-up body fall down its missing throat and rest inside its missing belly. If you are eaten by the gashadokuro, your mother will never pray over your crushed bones, because you will be swallowed straight into the other dimension where who-knows-what happens to your body and soul.

In all the smoke and fog my grandfather saw nothing anymore and thought maybe he had gotten away. Maybe the gashadokuro was satisfied with all the other bodies it found. There were so many. But grandfather never stopped crawling, as hard as he could, even if it was straight into the hands of the enemy. It's better to be shot, even tortured for years, than to be swallowed into a mysterious dimension by a skeleton of pure evil hunger. But trying his hardest did Grandpa no good. The gashadokuro appeared before him; Grandpa almost crawled into its mouth, in fact. My grandfather stopped just as he realized the rocks he was beginning to climb over were giant teeth. When he tried to jump back, gashadokuro picked him up by his jacket with its bony fingers. It lifted him high in the air and dangled him over its mouth like a grape. Below my grandfather there was no tongue, no throat, just teeth and bones and some invisible portal to take him straight to hell.

Grandpa woke up in the hospital tent. The army said that a mortar shell blew off his feet. Grandpa said it's not true. I have had many family members serve in the military. All of them went missing in action or came back with missing body parts and horrible stories like this one. If you're lucky, the spirit energy that holds the gashadokuro together will run out before it eats all of you. Better to live out life with one arm or no feet than to be a victim for eternity in the spirit dimension.

I know now that the gashadokuros have a taste for my bones and can smell my bloodline. Wherever there is suffering enough for them to animate they will follow my family and try to eat us. And I also know to be wary of ringing in my ears.

I never went to war. I will never go anywhere with great suffering, like to help the homeless or starving. I feel ashamed to be a selfish coward, but the gashadokuro have a taste for my bloodline. I will not go where the gashadokuro spirit is strong. And still, whenever I hear a ringing in my ears, just to be safe, I duck. It doesn't hurt to duck. And some nights I still sleep in a tight ball, with nothing sticking out, to not tempt the gashadokuro.

The Path to
Black Hands

The Path to Black Hands

People cannot memorize stories. Not exactly anyway. Certain geniuses or persons who specialize in memory can memorize long lists of words or extraordinarily large numbers, but these same people, given a story to memorize, will always recite the story differently. It's because the human brain doesn't save information like a computer. The brain saves new impressions based on old impressions, so stories always come out differently based on the teller's personal history. Sorry, I know this is very complicated, but it's necessary to understand because investigating the next story was very difficult. We have no direct evidence and it is the sort of thing where eyewitness accounts are normally unreliable. However, we have so many accounts that are told a certain way that people couldn't possibly be retelling stories they heard. There must be multiple firsthand accounts of this strange and dark being they call "Black Hands."

Imagine for a second that you are a martial artist and that you have been training at your gym. You love it, you love the martial arts. And because you love it, you train harder, and because you train harder you get better than others. Everyone starts to notice, they start commenting. It's nice, you're getting good at what you love. It's time to start competing and let people see what you can do. But then one day your coach holds you late to talk to you. No one else is around for this very strange conversation.

"What if I told you that there are two paths? You could go on and be a professional fighter. You're good already so you could get a shot at the fame. You'll date the hottest people. And you can get money, big house, everything... But you will never be the strongest fighter in the world. There's another path though. You will be a Nobody. You'll barely have two dimes to rub together in your pocket, no one will want you, and no one will know you except a handful of the same jerks. But in this world, you can truly see... and maybe even be... the strongest fighter in the world."

Well, most of the people who read this aren't fools. They would take the money and the popularity. Who cares about being the best if no one knows you're the best? But for some people the idea of being the true strongest is just too much. It's a drive that's a little more common in fighters. Not every occupation is a brutal battle to be the best. Being the best at fighting isn't like being the best at chess or piano. It relates to survival. These people who fight for their occupation feel the need to know how much they can survive. And they push it all the time to find out what they can take and increase what they can endure. But the ones who push the most are the very ones who end up in darkness.

They follow the coach's secret instructions, to Nowhere towns without airports, that they have to drive to, over long, long distances. Or to stinking, dirty alleys in foreign cities. Or sometimes, to prisons in the poorest and most corrupt countries. The fighter finally finds the right parking lot, or back entrance or wherever. They whisper why they came. Then this weird stranger looks them up and down; up and down.

One of these fighters, we'll call him Frederico, goes to this new place. And after some stranger looks him up and down, the stranger points to another guy. He tells Frederico to fight this person and Frederico does. And Frederico wins because he's very good at martial arts. He sort of embarrasses the other man. And everyone laughs, but Frederico gets the hunch that they're laughing at him. They tell him fight another... and another. Frederico wins and wins again. Frederico can move, he can hit hard, he can dance. But it becomes clearer and clearer that the audience is all laughing at him. Why are they laughing at him if he is winning? Finally he's beaten five guys in a row, something very exhausting and difficult. They give him some water and a snack. He's tired, but not too tired; he feels good. He says so.

Then they tell him he did a very good job. They'd like him to fight again. So they ask him to fight the first man he beat, one he beat pretty badly.

- C R A C K -

That's the moment when the world opens up like an earthquake in a movie. What Frederico thought was the real world breaks apart. And what's underneath, the real reality, swallows this fighter into something that he was never prepared for, NEVER.

Now when Frederico hits this man, it's like the man doesn't feel pain. The man doesn't get tired. And the man moves so much faster than Frederico that it's like he took a magic potion. This is what Frederico's coach meant by the path to the true strongest. This is not like anything Frederico ever saw on TV. They make him fight all the same fighters again. All of the fighters are like the first one; they toy with Frederico and not in an easy way. Frederico has a facial fracture, a bruise covering his entire left thigh, a sprained ankle, and invisible organ bruising. They went easy on him. They tell Frederico he did a great job and he can come back whenever he wants.

Some people disappear after this. They get their glimpse of the other side and they pull back to go be a carpenter or something. We never hear from them, they're probably afraid to tell anyone about it. We have only interviewed the ones who went full in. Make no mistake. Some do go all in, even though the pain is terrifying. It's not a lack of fear that makes them choose to stay on this path. It's that they're even more afraid of their weakness. They can't go away, knowing that there are others who are so much stronger than them. They have to try and get atleast a little bit stronger. And little by little they do.

They can't do real fights too much, especially early on; it takes too long to heal. But it changes everything about how they train. Speed isn't an advantage; speed is a necessity for survival. Stamina too. The toughness comes without trying. It comes from being hurt so bad that anything which doesn't break you is no different to your mind than an itch. Imagine a blow that knocks all of the air out of you, only feeling like an itch.

Frederico heard certain stories and comments many times without understanding them. It takes a few months for fighters to piece together when the others are talking about Black Hands. First Frederico thought it was just about their hands getting dirty from fighting. Then he thought it was some kind of disease, like a fungus, the way they were afraid of Black Hands. Finally he realized Black Hands was a person... or a kind of person.

Black Hands, they say, came from an older religion, one with many gods, not these newer ones with one super god, or anything like that. He came from a religion with many dark gods who fought many gods of the heavens. And the dark gods created Black Hands as their hero of war. He was made to fight the heroes of the heavens and even the gods themselves. As light and science spread on the world, these older gods disappeared. But Black Hands was so deep in the shadows, so tightly tucked in the crevices that he survived for eons. He is still here because he lived out of the reach of light and science. And people who wander too far from the reach of light and science can meet him. And when they do, they will test strength and survival in a way that they never meant.

Frederico was on this path. He didn't exactly want it; he only sort of understood it. But even if he fully understood he couldn't turn back. The addiction to strength, the fear of weakness, was too much. And when he finally got strong enough to try another place, they would tell him where to go: other countries, certain prison blocks. His life was hell.

He had a girlfriend once in the beginning. She got jealous when she heard he was leaving her to train somewhere else, so she tried to kill him by throwing a venomous snake in his bed. Frederico lay in bed dying. There was no one to rescue him. Nobody knew him but that girl and the other fighters. He thought of crying out for a stranger to take him to the doctor. But he didn't have money for a doctor so he didn't bother. He survived by luck, or maybe because his training had somehow made him stronger.

After he survived the snakebite, he started training with snakes for speed. Another fighter helped him get some venomous snakes and Frederico practiced trying to grab them without getting bit. His hands became quicker than a mongoose, but he got bit alot in this training too.

Frederico also needed body speed, so he fought panthers, and often lost. Slashed and bitten, someone had to pull the panther off by a rope. And when Frederico healed enough, he asked to try again. Everything that you and I are afraid to face, Frederico was afraid not to face. He was afraid any weakness might cost him a fight. He built his tolerance to pain. He saw an Internet video of a man getting bitten and stung by the most painful insects on the planet so he copy-catted. He got bitten by spiders and ants, stung by scorpions and wasps. And he still fought other men like him. They tore his muscles in fights so he stretched until he tore his muscles himself; better than happening in a fight. His arms often got dislocated.

He got so many dislocations that after a while he didn't always notice when it happened. He's not the only one who trained in crazy ways. And some fighters maimed or killed themselves with their own training.

But Frederico was becoming a name in the underworld, still a Nobody to the outside world. But if he showed up to a new underground place and asked to fight, no one went easy on him, no one laughed when he won. There got to be fewer recommendations for places he could go and more and more mentions of Black Hands. Everyone knew that Black Hands would come for him. They just didn't know when and they didn't think Frederico would come back to tell them the story. The better a fighter got, the worse their chances became. The closer you are to Black Hands's strength, the harder he is on you. Second- and third-tier fighters often survived their encounters, maybe with a broken back, broken legs, or a delirious fever. But they lived and could tell others the story of Black Hands. But the top-tier fighters, most often, were left dead. Frederico was already the top tier. In fact he could become the strongest in the world.

Frederico was going to a new place, a long maze of an alley in Beijing, China. Frederico saw a man go down into the dark alley before him. The man was large and muscular, larger than Frederico, but that meant little. The stranger's eyes were glowing, evil-like, and his body gave off an eerie aura of orange vapors rising off like steam. Frederico was used to it, he wasn't shocked. Many did everything they could to compete in this world. People took steroids, used dangerous drugs, even got organ transplants: eyes that see better, glands that produce more adrenaline, bigger heart and lungs. Frederico never did any of this; he had no money for it, besides he felt that such tricks would make him weaker in the end. For those that could not find enough strength in the dark side of science, there was witchcraft; spells from other religions left over from dark ages;

spells hidden in deep chinks of stone like catacombs under the foundations of the modern world, hidden deep enough in the damp and dirty earth to survive still, survive the science and the light, just like Black Hands did. The glowing stranger had surely summoned the power of some nation's old gods. Maybe he did it just for his fight with Frederico.

Frederico did fight that glowing man and he lost. Frederico didn't lose because the other man had witchcraft though, he lost because he had aches and weakness that slowed him down. Frederico had been on the path for so long that he got old.

Oldness doesn't work the way young people imagine, it's not a hill you go over. Many parts are still getting stronger while other things are getting weaker. Frederico could still get stronger, but at the same time he would be getting weaker. He may have reached his peak.

The peak is what Black Hands was waiting for. Black Hands had been watching him. Frederico didn't know because Black Hands doesn't watch by hanging out in the audience and seeing. Black Hands watches from the dark magic cracks in alleys at night. Black Hands watched and knew that Frederico was at his peak. So if Black hands wanted the best fight possible, he would have to challenge Frederico now.

Frederico went to another fight. He won. He beat a man who had started with dark science and moved to dark magic, but still was not stronger than Frederico. The audience had already disbursed. Frederico was walking out of the alley alone, no one staying to treat him like a celebrity, exactly what he was used to. Out of a pool of blood, Black Hands began to emerge. That is how he always emerged, the only way he could come out and challenge a mortal. Frederico didn't see it, but other fighters we've interviewed have seen it. Black Hands tapped Frederico on the shoulder and challenged him.

When Frederico saw, he knew instantly that it was Black Hands. He would have known it even if the strange man were wearing gloves. His skin was inhuman, grayish, bluish, whitish. His eyes shimmered and reflected like a dog's or cat's in the night, but silver in color. His body was skinny, much leaner than Frederico's, but not weak looking. Everything on the body was pure sinew, you could see every stringy line of muscle showing through, every tendon and vein. His hair was long and black and damp, and hung down in the way of his face. But his hands and wrists were black, as if dipped in ink or paint, pure black.

There, in the alley, with no one to watch, they fought, possibly the strongest fighter in the world and the hero of ancient, evil gods. It was a good match. They moved the same speed. They hit with the same power. They took hits as if they were made of stone. But Black Hands had dark powers. His hands must have been black with poison. The touch of them is said to cause searing pain and necrosis. But Frederico had trained with so many venomous snakes and spiders that he was immune to almost all poisons now and the hands did not hurt him. Black Hands breathed poisonous spores, but Frederico had slept so many times out in the woods by poisonous mushrooms, and in polluted alleys, that the breath didn't hurt him either. It seemed like Frederico really had a chance.

But Frederico slowly, slowly tired and Black Hands never did. Frederico saw it happening and he laughed a nervous laugh.

Certain people... laugh when something goes wrong. Like a certain type of kid might fall out of a tree and break her leg and laugh hysterically because she doesn't know what else to do. That's what Frederico's laugh was. He noticed his own fatigue, he knew he would wind down and when he wound down he would be killed. But it's the path he chose so there was nothing else he could do... but laugh.

When Frederico laughed, something happened to Black Hands. Black Hands's strength derived from the fear in his enemies. And laughter was his weakness. Suddenly Black Hands was tired. His attacks slowed down, and Frederico came back. And when Frederico saw this demon getting tired and weak, he thought that was really funny so he laughed more. Black Hands got weaker and couldn't defend himself. Frederico became more and more brutal; he broke Black Hands's arms and legs. But Black Hands could still take pain and he didn't fall down from things like that. Black Hands was so weakened that Frederico caught him in a headlock and !CRACK! broke his neck, twisting his head all the way around backwards. Frederico dropped Black Hands to the dirty ground of the alley, dead in a puddle.

He stood over the body looking for a few seconds, but there was nothing to do. He wouldn't report the body to anyone, he wouldn't bury it. Frederico just walked away down the alley, the strongest fighter in the world. After he went a few steps he heard behind him, "Good job." He turned and saw silver eyes shining at him through the darkness. He turned around and kept walking.

Some of the fighters we interviewed said they didn't believe the claim that Black Hands had been beaten until they had Frederico tell them in person, eye-to-eye. Then they would all swear he was telling the truth. We can't confirm Frederico's part of the story, but our psychology algorithms show that the fighters all talk about Black Hands with details consistent with someone who has really seen something instead of retelling a rumor. Black Hands still emerges from blood puddles to challenge fighters and will probably continue to do so until the light and science can find him and purge him from this world.

The easiest way to live your life is to stay away from the dark, stay where science and society light up everything. But if you do go into the dark, go so deep, and become so strong, that you can survive the darkness.

CPSIA information can be obtained
at www.ICGtesting.com
Printed in the USA
BVHW031138021020
590172BV00001B/47